LUCY

TYLER

Praise for *Tyler & Lucy are the Best of Friends*

"A delicate and caring young storybook that introduces how friends become, and stay, friends. *Tyler & Lucy* reinforces that friendships take time, time filled with adventures to experience. There are great amounts of short text to give the little one thinking-time to take it all in, along with complementary illustrations that a young child will love."
—Elizabeth Thomas of @tigerlilybookseducators Instagram Book Reviewer

"If you are looking for a heart-warming story of family and friendship, then look no further as *Tyler & Lucy are the Best of Friends* is just that! Based on a real-life tale of two inseparable playmates, this book will give you that warm and fuzzy feeling that comes from reading a story filled with love. Not only is the prose a pleasure to read, but the illustrations are also charming and fun. An excellent read and a lovely account of two best friends' journey through life together. Their delightful bond proves that dogs really are man's (and baby's!) best friend."
—Fiona Phimister of @whatwillowread Instagram/Blog Book Reviewer

"Heartwarming! An endearing story of a boy and his dog. Tyler and Lucy will touch our heart. This picture book beautifully portrays the special animal-child bond found between Tyler and Lucy...sharing love and joy with us all!"
—Christine Gallo of @the_childrens_library @thevintagechildrenslibrary
Reviewer/Curator

"A lovely book exploring the bond between a child and a pet! Well-illustrated to clearly show the love between Tyler and Lucy and the fun the two of them have together. Makes a lovely bedtime read."
—Katherine Broad of @therightbookdevon Instagram Book Reviewer

"A sweet little story about the joy of a child learning and growing along with a furry companion. This book will remind readers of their own special moments with their pets and maybe even make them want to add another best friend to the family!"
—Jenna Nelson of @bookshelvesmatter Instagram Book Reviewer

To my Sweet Peanut and my Beanie Girl,
Thank you for inspiring me to capture the adorable, loving, comical, and sometimes mischievous relationship you two share. Watching your bond develop has brought so much fun and happiness to our family. Mommy loves you both with all her heart.

To my amazingly supportive and encouraging husband,
Thank you for always pushing me to follow my passions and strive for my dreams. Without you this book would never have come to fruition. I love you so much.

www.mascotbooks.com

Tyler & Lucy are the Best of Friends

For more information, please contact:
Mascot Books
620 Herndon Parkway #320
Herndon, VA 20170
info@mascotbooks.com

Library of Congress Control Number: 2017918639

CPSIA Code: PBANG0218A
ISBN-13: 978-1-68401-647-1

Printed in the United States

Tyler & Lucy are the Best of Friends

Alicia Arso-DiStefano

illustrated by Alejandra Lopez

This is a story about a
boy named Tyler and his dog Lucy.

Lucy loved her new baby human from the day Mommy and Daddy brought Tyler home. She enjoyed playing with children, but she never had a baby of her own to love and play with. Lucy was so excited! Her tail would not stop wagging!

When Mommy and Daddy carried Tyler around the house, Lucy followed right behind, making sure her little friend was safe and happy.

Lucy loved cuddling up with baby Tyler. She nuzzled his face with her snout and his tiny hands would reach for her fluffy gray fur. Lucy enjoyed the snuggling, but she couldn't wait for her little friend to be big enough to play.

As Tyler grew, so did their friendship. The bigger Tyler got, the more fun he and Lucy could have together.

When Tyler was big enough, the two friends spent hours rolling around on a large, soft blanket playing with their toys.

Lucy ran around with her favorite squeaky toy, Sheepy, and Tyler giggled and squealed with delight every time!

The two friends shared an afternoon snack every day.
Tyler would sneak Lucy bits of whatever he was eating.
Their favorite snack was strawberries.

Tyler even let Lucy have some of his bottle when Mommy wasn't looking.

Whenever Tyler cried, Lucy would hurry to bring him Monkey, his favorite stuffed animal, to cheer him up.

Then she would give him sloppy wet kisses on his rosy red cheeks until he was happy again.

yler quickly learned to crawl and Lucy followed him round to make sure he didn't get into any trouble.

Sometimes they couldn't help but get into mischief. Playin
in Mommy's baking cabinet, getting sugar and flour all
over the place, was definitely a lot of fun!

After all of the excitement they had each day, Tyler and Lucy were always very tired when bedtime came around

At the end of every day, they loved snuggling up together on Mommy's lap for their bedtime stories.

When Mommy and Daddy tucked Tyler into his crib, Lucy always curled up beside him on her own little bed.

The two sleepy heads
drifted off, dreaming
about the adventures of
the new day to come.
Tyler and Lucy are the
best of friends.

The real Tyler and Lucy!

Have a book idea?

Contact us at:

info@mascotbooks.com | www.mascotbooks.com